"BOO-TiFUL

➤━━ A Spooky Cute Coloring Book ━➤━➤

Colored by
Fang-tastic Artist

Sustainilbilty Pledge:

This book is like a magical genie that appears only when you call for it! No wasted paper or dusty storerooms here. Designed by us, printed by Amazon at a facility nearest to you, giving a high-five to your local economy!

Paper Choice:

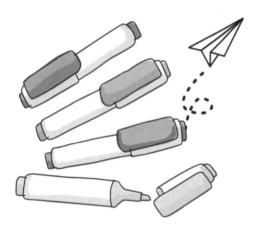

Given the limited paper choice from amazon we opted for the budget friendly standard paper, 50-61 pound (74-90 GSM) white paper for affordability and versatility. Note that paper weight varies based on printing location, so its best to pop in an extra sheet behind your coloring page when diving into markers or watery mediums. Big thanks for rolling with our paper pick! ♥

Before you begin:

Amazon's paper is optimal for soft pencil colors like polychromos or chalk pastels and alcohol-based brush tip markers. Swatch your colors on the Color Test Page to see how they deposit & bleed-through. Darker shades may bleed more than lighter ones. When using wet color mediums, place a blank sheet behind the page you're working on to keep the colorful chaos in check.

Dear Colorist,

Thank you for buying from an independent publisher.

If you have a minute to spare, we would love an honest review or rating.

Genuine insights from customers like you help us grow and also help others make the right purchase. Or you can simply choose a star rating.

Hope you enjoy coloring this book.

Happy Coloring!

SCAN ME!

Coloring Nook on Amazon

To explore the entire range of coloring books by COLORING NOOK on Amazon

‹‹ **scan this with your phone camera to explore.**

Like-Follow-Share

When you share your colored pages on Instagram please tag us. We would love to celebrate your artwork and add you to our global community of colorists. Lets support and grow with each other through our art.

scan this with your phone camera to follow us on insta ››

SCAN ME!

@COLORINGNOOK_BOOKS

BEFORE YOU BEGIN COLORING

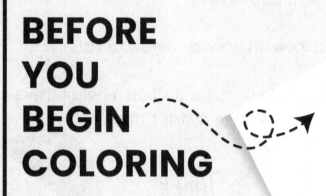

Place a thick sheet of paper behind the page you are coloring.

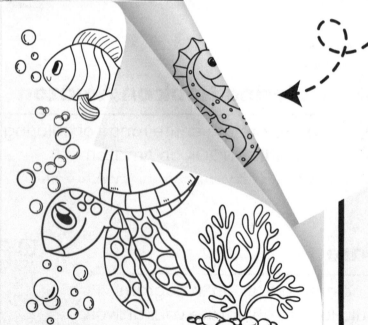

48 COLOR SWATCH

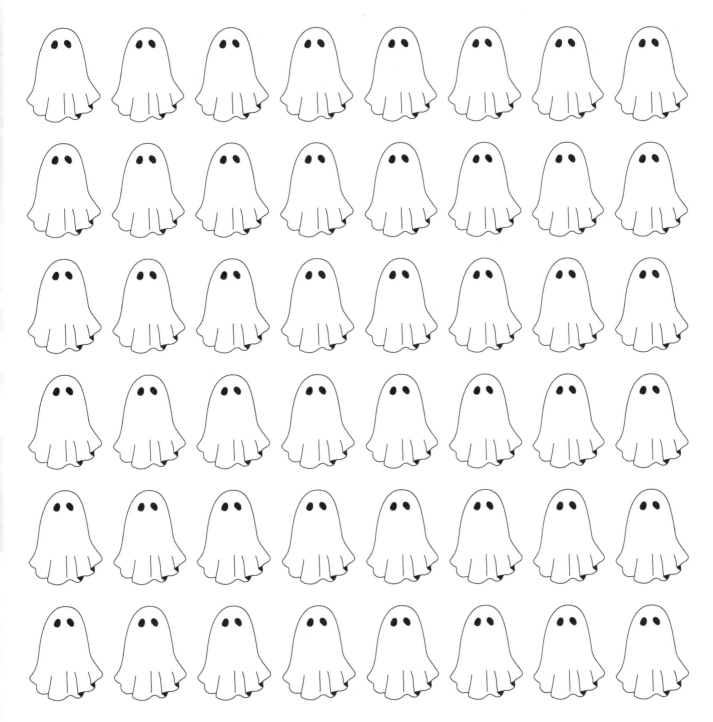

COLOR TEST PAGE

Test your colors to check how they look on this paper. Place an extra sheet behind.

Made in United States
Troutdale, OR
08/21/2024

22202313R10033